DOUG

THE BUG THAT WENT BOING!

For all the wonderful staff and children
at Blueberry Nursery

SIMON & SCHUSTER
First published in Great Britain in 2013
by Simon & Schuster UK Ltd
1st Floor, 222 Gray's Inn Road, London, WC1X 8HB
A CBS Company

A CIP catalogue record for this book is available
from the British Library upon request

978-1-4711-1908-8 (HB)
978-1-4711-7869-6 (PB)
978-1-4711-1844-9 (eBook)

Printed in China
1 3 5 7 9 10 8 6 4 2

DOUG
THE BUG THAT WENT BOING!

by Sue Hendra and Paul Linnet

SIMON & SCHUSTER
London   New York   Sydney   Toronto   New Delhi

Doug and Trevor had been best friends for a long time. They played together every day and didn't like to be apart.

One day they were playing Berry Ball when . . .

Oh dear.

"Bad luck, Trevor," said Doug.
"It's your turn to get it down."

"Is not," said Trevor.

"Is too," said Doug.

"Is NOT!" said Trevor.

"You always make me climb up there," said Doug, crossly. "You always say it's my turn when it's not. I don't want to play any more."

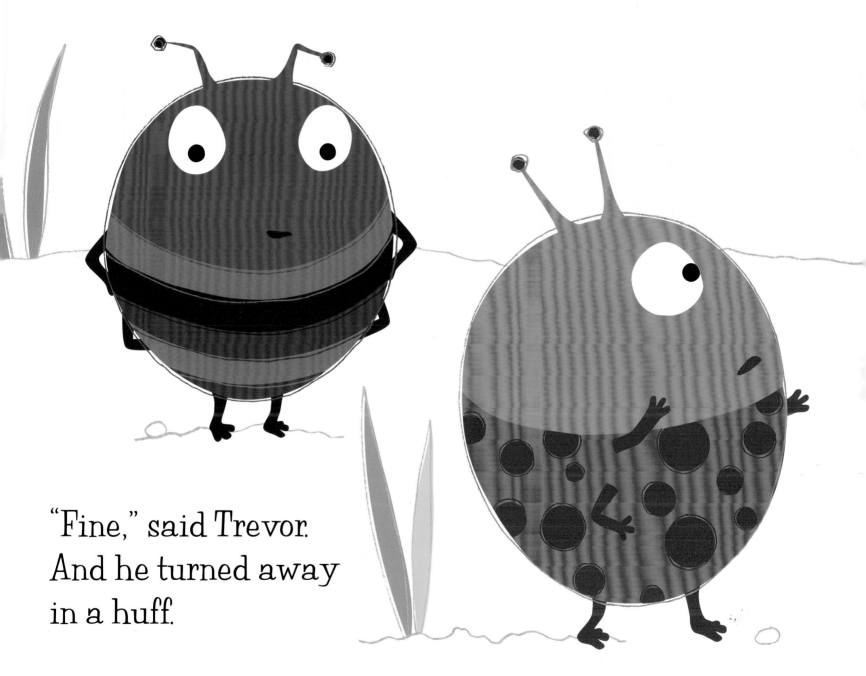

"Fine," said Trevor.
And he turned away
in a huff.

But just then . . .

... a great big shovel came
down and scooped Doug up.

Oh no!

What on earth was happening?

"Doug!"

cried Trevor.

"Trevor!" cried Doug.

When he finally opened his eyes,
Doug got quite a surprise.

"TREVOR!" he yelled. "HELP!"

But Trevor was too far away to hear him

"I've got to get home,"
thought Doug. But how?

Then he heard a funny noise.

Bzzzz, bzzzz, bump!

It was a very dizzy fly. He was banging his head against the window.

Bzzzz, bzzzz, bump!

"Erm, maybe you should try the door," said Doug, politely.

"The door? Great idea! Why didn't I think of that? I've been here for days. Oh, how can I ever thank you?" said the fly.

Doug tried not to laugh. "Well," he said, "maybe you could take me with you?"

"I'll try," said the fly. "You look quite heavy. But here goes!"

Bzzzz, bzzzz . . .

...whoa!

"Don't drop me in there!" cried Doug.

Bzzzz, bzzzz . . .

...whey!

"Or on there!" he gasped.

"And definitely **don't**
drop me THERE!"

Phew! That was close.

But the fly was starting to wobble.
"Don't ... think ... I ... can ...
hold ... on ..."

And then -

PLOP!
Doug landed, SPLAT,
in somebody's breakfast.

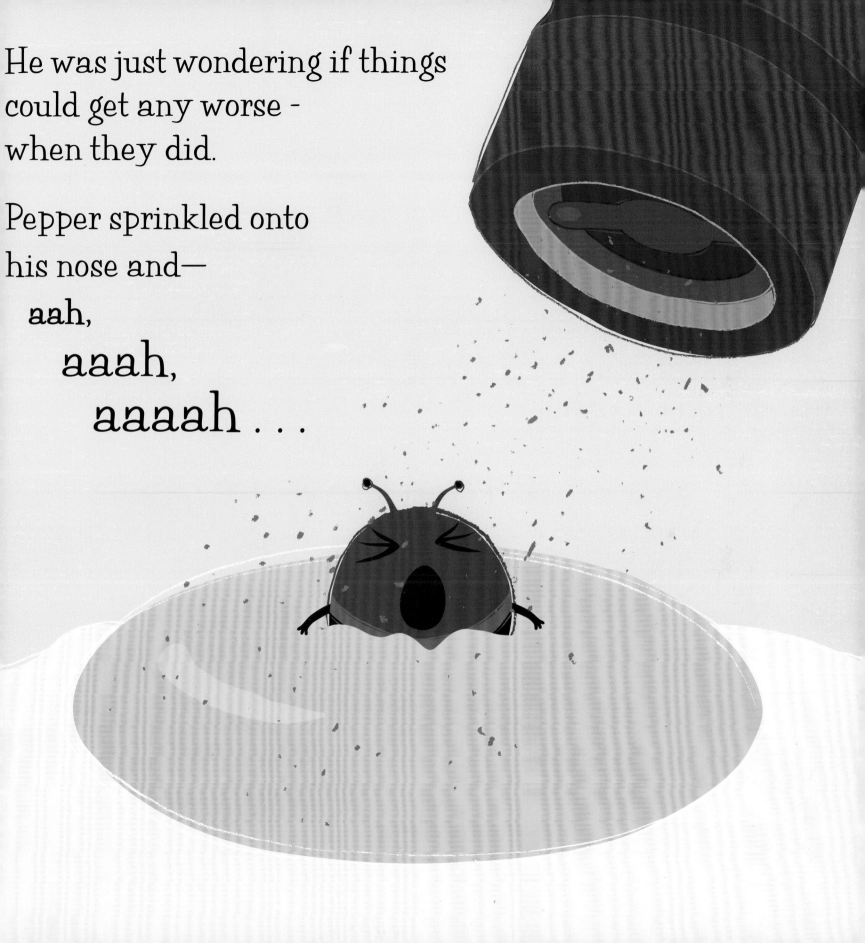

He was just wondering if things could get any worse - when they did.

Pepper sprinkled onto his nose and—

aah,

aaah,

aaaah . . .

...choo!

Doug shot through the air
and span round and round
on the ceiling fan.

Then **boing!**

He bounced off a sponge cake

boing!

boing!

boing!

nd popped up a pedal bin

SUPER BOING!

which sent him spinning through the air -

. . . towards the toaster.

Ping!

He smashed through the toast
and began to fall.

He grabbed the first thing he could
and swung—

aargh!—

all the way back . . .

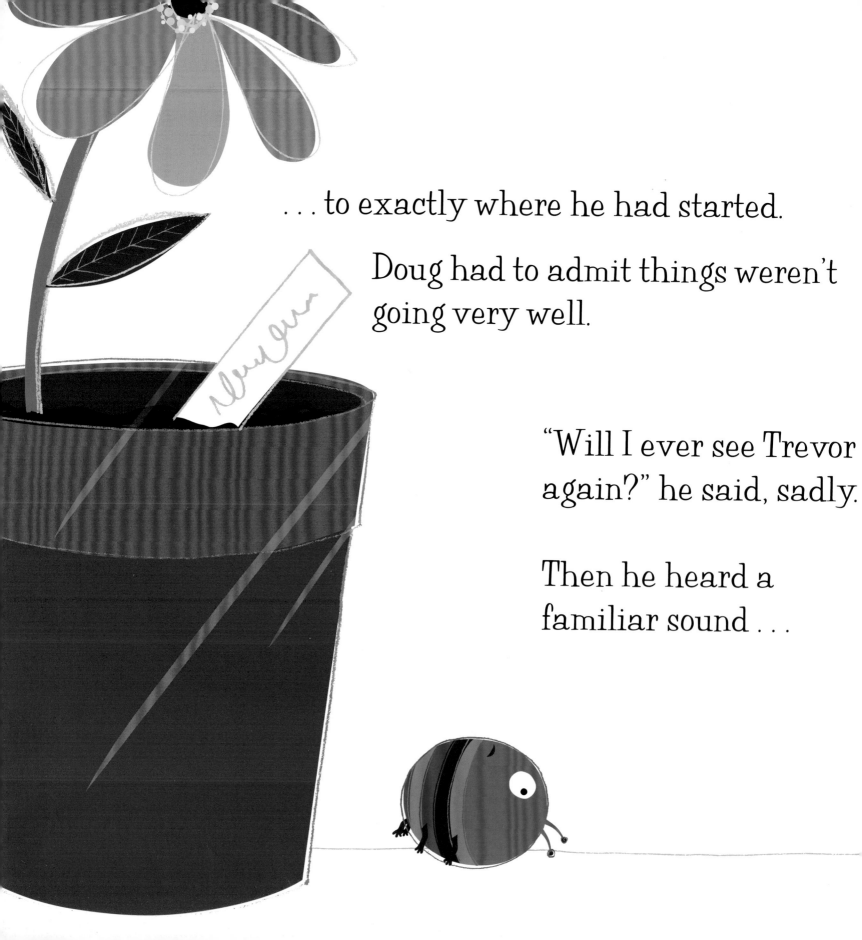

. . . to exactly where he had started.

Doug had to admit things weren't going very well.

"Will I ever see Trevor again?" he said, sadly.

Then he heard a familiar sound . . .

"Bzzzz, bzzzz, byeeeee!" it called.
It was the fly, buzzing out of sight.
And that was when Doug noticed
that the window ... WAS OPEN!

"Hey! Wait for me!" he called.
How was he going to get out now?

Then Doug had an idea ...

Wheeeee!

"Home I go!"
cried Doug.

The friends were so happy to see each other again.
"I'm sorry I wouldn't get the ball," said Trevor.
"I'm sorry I got so cross," said Doug.
"Tell you what," said Trevor. "How about
a game of Berry Ball right now?"
"You're on!" said Doug.

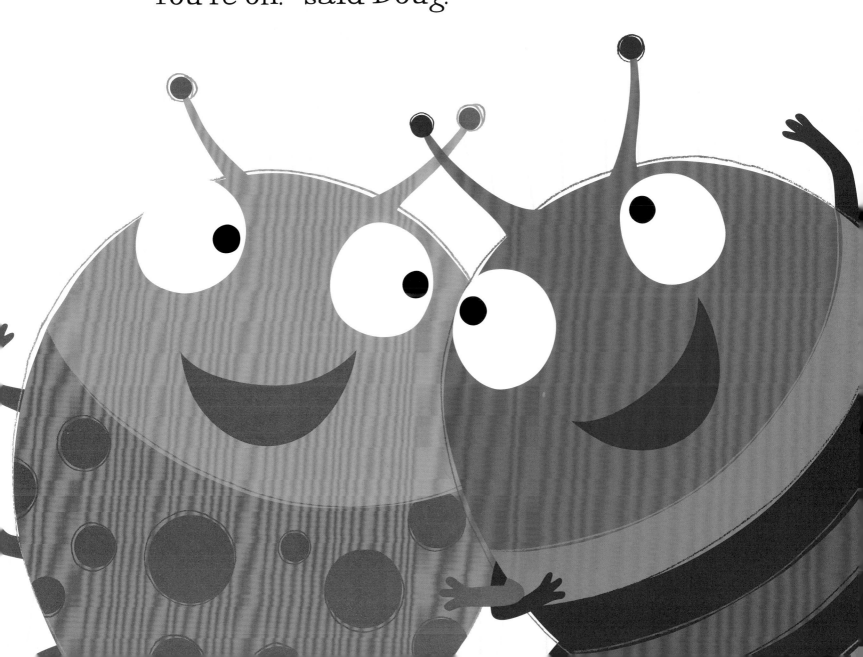

And all was well until . . .

oh no!
It happened again!

Doug looked at Trevor.
Trevor looked at Doug.

"I'll get it," said Trevor.

"Let me," said Doug.

"No, no, it's definitely
my turn," said Trevor.

And they were so busy arguing,
they didn't hear a familiar sound.

Bzzzz, bzzzz . . .

"CATCH!"
said the fly.

And they all played happily till the sun went down.